T0082943

THE RECRUITMENT

R O N A L D   E .   E S T E S

iUniverse

THE RECRUITMENT

iUniverse books may be ordered through booksellers or by contacting:

iUniverse
1663 Liberty Drive
Bloomington, IN 47403
www.iuniverse.com
844-349-9409

Because of the dynamic nature of the Internet, any web addresses or links contained in this book may have changed since publication and may no longer be valid. The views expressed in this work are solely those of the author and do not necessarily reflect the views of the publisher, and the publisher hereby disclaims any responsibility for them.

Any people depicted in stock imagery provided by Getty Images are models, and such images are being used for illustrative purposes only. Certain stock imagery © Getty Images.

ISBN: 978-1-6632-3558-9 (sc)
ISBN: 978-1-6632-3560-2 (hc)
ISBN: 978-1-6632-3559-6 (e)

Library of Congress Control Number: 2022902140

Print information available on the last page.

iUniverse rev. date: 02/01/2022

PROLOGUE

For forty-four years, the Soviet Union and the United States were locked in a geopolitical, ideological, and economic struggle: the Cold War. The two principal adversaries, the Soviet KGB and the American CIA, waged a daily struggle to learn the plans and capabilities of each other's country and to engage in covert action to deprive their opponent of influence and ideological dominance throughout the world. The two intelligence services did not attack each other directly, both of them fearing the consequences of the resultant worldwide assassinations and kidnappings. The KGB, however, had a history of passing on to terrorist organizations the identities and home addresses of CIA officers. The primary target of each intelligence service was the recruitment of penetration agents in the other's service. This story is about how one CIA station pursued that objective during the last decade of the Cold War.

CHAPTER 1

The ritual began at six.

At the end of the working day each Friday, all five case officers in the Soviet section of the CIA Beirut station gathered in the office of their chief to hold what was known to them as the Friday-Evening Vespers. They sat on the sofa and the overstuffed chairs around the coffee table. The secretary entered with a tray holding six glasses and a quart of vodka that, since the previous Friday, had been kept in the freezer in the vault adjoining their office suite. She placed a glass on the table in front of each man and filled it with vodka. Without a word, she left the room with the bottle. She knew the routine. The embassy of the United States of America did not sanction drinking alcohol in its offices, but the Vespers were sanctified.

The section chief, Brooks Moss, raised his glass and said, "Gentlemen, a toast. Thank God it's Friday—only two more working days until Monday."

Jack Duncan, sitting on the sofa opposite Moss, smiled through his thick, drooping black mustache. "For God's sake,

Brooksie, you've made that same damned toast every Vespers for over two years," he said. "Can't you think of anything else to say?"

"And why are we *gentlemen* at every Vespers and *you damn people* all week long?" asked Peter Falin, one of the station's Russian speakers, sitting at the end of the coffee table.

All the men chuckled.

"Because, gentlemen, I like you a lot better on Friday evenings than I do on Monday mornings. And you all look better after a drink of vodka."

Moss took a pack of cigarettes and a lighter from the side pocket of his suit coat and tossed them on the coffee table. He lit a cigarette, looking around the table at the faces of these men he was so fond of. "But this evening's Vespers is not going to be the typical session of raucous alcoholic overindulgence to which you all are so attached. I want to discuss the Soviet target. We've hit the wall on Gromov. We've been after him for six months, and during that time, we've surveilled him for over eight weeks. We've tapped his phone, put audio in his house, and ran three access agents into him. Louie here"—he pointed to the case officer at the left end of the sofa—"has had dinner with him twice and one all-night drinking session. And we haven't come up with anything. He loves his wife, doesn't hate his father, seems to be doing well in his KGB career, and thinks Stalin wasn't such a bad guy. He's a Marxist and believes socialism will triumph over Western decadence. We've got nothing to work with. I want to drop him as a target. He is not recruitable—at least not at this point in his life. Anybody disagree?" He leaned back in his chair and looked around the table. "Louie, it's your case. Do you agree?"

"Yeah," Louie said, "let's bag it. I don't like the guy anyway."

Everyone at the table nodded.

"OK. We've picked a new target," Moss said. "Jack and I have been talking about this for over a week." Pointing to Duncan, he said, "You take it, Jack. Give us a rundown."

Duncan picked up a legal-size yellow pad he had laid on the coffee table and, reading from it, said, "His name is Alexandr Alekseyevich Petrov. His friends call him Sasha. He's forty-one years old, KGB, First Chief Directorate. Married with two children: a son, twelve years old, who studies in Moscow during the school year but spends his summers here with his parents, and a daughter, seven, who lives with them. I have their names, but you guys don't care about that. His wife's name is Tamara. His father is KGB, maybe retired—we don't know—and was, or is, pretty high up, but we're not sure what rank he was. Our Petrov is an Arabist and has served four years in Damascus and three years in Cairo, but he also speaks English and French. His first tour abroad was Paris, where he stayed four years. We've had some people in contact with Petrov through the years. Nothing serious—cocktail parties and a couple of dinner parties—but our guys found him convivial, good sense of humor, drinks well, and has a penchant for single-malt Scotch whiskey. That's about it, Brooksie. We don't know a hell of a lot about him. Oh, one more thing. His wife is attractive, speaks French and English well, and they seem very compatible. They hold hands in public—things like that."

"Do we know where he lives?" Moss asked.

"No, and he's not in the phone book."

"Do we have a photograph of him?"

"Yes," Duncan replied. From the inside pocket of his tweed blazer, he took out a three-by-four photograph and laid it on the table. It was a four-year-old picture of Petrov and his wife shopping in a souk in Cairo. It had been taken from about six feet away, full face, so their features were clear. Duncan passed it around the table.

"Well, what do you think?" Moss asked, looking around.

"Why not?" said Tom Whiteside, another of the station's Russian-speaking officers, sitting to the left of Duncan on the couch. "He seems as good as any other Soviet target we don't know anything about. At least he drinks good whiskey."

"I second that," Falin said with a crooked smile. "I mean, about him being a target—not the whiskey. Let's have a whack at him."

Everyone at the table nodded in agreement.

"Good. We'll start tomorrow," Moss said, lighting another cigarette.

The secretary entered the office with the vodka bottle and refilled all the glasses.

"Ay, Ellie, young wan, you've a bright future in this organization," said John Patrick O'Shea, sitting at the end of the coffee table, facing Falin.

"Thank you, John Patrick, but I will not leave the bottle on the table," said Ellie, smiling as she left the office.

"All right. Louie, contact the surveillance team tonight," Moss said. "Enlarge that photograph and pass it out to them. Petrov will probably go to the embassy tomorrow morning for half a day. See if the team can pick him up as he leaves and follow him home. Make sure they stay with him until they put him to bed each night. We'll want to know who he spends his free time with this weekend. Tell them to case his apartment building for the names and whatever they can get about the people whose apartments have a common wall with his. Don't forget the apartment across the hall. If that's available, we can put an access agent in it. Should they miss him tomorrow, try again Monday. Pick him up as he leaves the embassy for the day and stay with him for three days. Also get a new photograph. Then we'll regroup and see what we have. Any questions? Any ideas?"

No one spoke.

"OK. Jack, you'll be the lead case officer on this. Why

don't you come in tomorrow and go over recent Soviet Embassy phone-tap transcripts? See if you can come up with people he's calling from the embassy and who's been calling him. Let's see what kind of contacts he has around town."

"Will do."

"All right. Let's get Ellie in here for one more round, and then we'll call it quits. I'll be here in the morning and around all weekend."

Brooks Moss sat at his desk long after everyone else had departed. He had planned this meeting for weeks. *Someday,* he had thought, *I will tell these men of my introduction to operations against the KGB—but not yet.* He wanted to tell them of the night he remembered so vividly of sixteen years ago, when as a junior case officer, he had driven a CIA car through Checkpoint Charlie, that gate in the Berlin Wall between West and East Berlin, with a fellow case officer sitting beside him in the front seat and another in the back seat.

Under the back seat, a hinged panel allowed a person to lie on the floor and roll under the seat to be concealed. After showing the case officers' diplomatic passports and being waved through the checkpoint by the East German border guards, Moss had taken the microphone of the push-to-talk radio concealed in the dashboard and said, "Able one."

The radio crackled, and a voice answered, "Roger."

He then sped rapidly down the dimly lit and mostly deserted boulevard for three blocks and turned right.

The case officer in the back seat barked, "Pull over, stop, and turn your lights off."

No car entered the street behind them. They started again, took the first left, then the next right, and again pulled to the curb and turned the lights off. There was no surveillance. Moss then moved the car forward about twenty meters with the lights off, turned into an alley, and stopped in front of the second doorway. When a man dressed in a trench coat emerged, the case officer in the back seat opened the back door and said in English, "Get in, lie on the floor, roll under the seat, and keep silent."

When the man disappeared under the back seat, Moss gunned the engine and sped out of the alley, turned the lights on, took the microphone from the dashboard, and said, "Baker one."

"Roger."

Moss then drove back to Checkpoint Charlie and passed into West Berlin.

The Russian stayed with the three case officers all that night and most of the next day in a CIA safe house. The next night, they returned him to East Berlin, again concealed under the back seat.

For the next twenty months, until Moss was transferred from Berlin to Geneva, Moss drove the car into East Berlin twice a month to pick up the KGB officer, take him to a safe house for a meeting, and drive him back to East Berlin. Over the course of the meetings, Moss was introduced to the KGB officer and participated in the conversations along with the other two case officers. The Soviet was a lieutenant colonel in the KGB and the deputy chief of the KGB *Rezidentura* (station) in East Berlin. He was a valuable agent. He briefed the CIA officers on all the rezidentura operations, identified all their German agents, and provided copies of the rezidentura correspondence with KGB headquarters in Moscow. The man had spoken English fluently after studying the language in Moscow and serving two tours in London. Moss had liked the man, and they'd become quite friendly.

Moss yearned to tell his case officers about the operation in Berlin. But CIA regulations forbade his revealing to uninvolved personnel the details of operations and the identities of agents except for on a need-to-know basis.

CHAPTER 2

Louie Martelli walked out of the embassy and put on dark glasses, squinting into the last rays of the sun as the red ball slowly disappeared into the Mediterranean Sea. The upper floors of the pastel-colored apartment buildings lining the Corniche were bathed in a rich golden light.

Martelli crossed the Corniche, the avenue in West Beirut that rims the eastern shore of the Mediterranean, and got into his car.

Luigi Antonio Martelli, known as Louie outside his family, came from a family of vintners. His father, an uncle, and an older brother owned and operated a modest winery, founded by Luigi's great-grandfather, on twenty-seven acres in California's Napa Valley. In the 1960s, Luigi's father had replaced their vines with merlot, and although the resulting wines were not top of the line, the family made a good living selling them to larger houses for blending.

Luigi's father, Antonio, a tall, sinewy man with laughing eyes and curly black hair sprinkled with gray, had always dreamed that both of his sons would join him on the family land. But although Luigi always enjoyed drinking the product of the family's harvests, he hated the making of it.

After years of arguing, cajoling, and pleading, and much intervention from his wife, Tony Martelli finally gave his youngest son, Luigi, a tearful embrace and a kiss on each cheek and sent him off to Stanford. Luigi stayed at the university long enough to earn a master's degree in Middle Eastern studies and to meet the girl he would marry after graduation.

Now Louie had been a CIA case officer for almost ten years. He and Mary had two children: Antonio, seven, and Maria, four. After completing the year of training that the Directorate of Operations requires for all case officers, Louie had been assigned to the Near East Division. Soon after, the division sent him to a two-year Arabic-language course. The first year of that drudgery, at the CIA headquarters' language school, was a precursor to a second year of training in Tunisia. Louie was a good linguist and finished high in his class. He was then thrilled to receive orders to join the CIA station in Kuwait for a three-year assignment. His dreams of becoming the second Lawrence of Arabia were dashed when the first time he got within three feet of a camel it attempted to bite him. The popular visions of camels moving effortlessly and gracefully over barren deserts were fraudulent, he decided. To him, the expression "graceful camel" was an oxymoron.

He was just beginning his third year in Beirut and

had spent the first eighteen months working to penetrate Palestinian terrorist organizations. He still handled three penetration agents, but for the last seven months, he had been working for Brooks Moss and the Soviet section.

I love Brooks Moss, and I love this job, he thought to himself as he looked in his rearview mirror.

Louie slowly moved his car from the curb and into the light traffic going south on the Corniche. Some six blocks farther, he parked in front of the Riviera Hotel. After bounding up the few steps that led to the lobby, he entered an alcove on the left, where he edged his way into one of the three telephone booths that lined one wall and closed the folding door.

After he inserted a coin and dialed, a female voice answered.

"Mary, honey," he said, "I'll be a little late. I've got something to do before I come home."

"Oh, Louie, the children have eaten, and I planned for us to eat at eight," Mary said. "Will you be very late?"

"No, I'll try to get there before nine."

"All right, but if you're much later, you'll miss the children before they go to bed."

"No, no, I'll make it. Keep them up. Bye-bye, gotta run. Love you," he said and hung up.

He placed a second coin and dialed again.

A voice on the other end said, "Nam?"

"Ba'ad Sa'a" (in one hour), Louie said and hung up.

He left the hotel and returned to his car. Fumbling with

his keys, he quickly glanced both ways on the Corniche to see whether there were any cars parked with men sitting in them. Spotting a taxi in front of the hotel with three men in it, he instinctively memorized the license number. In his car, Louie continued south on the Corniche and stayed on it as it curved east until he turned left on Rue de Bahrein. In his rearview mirror, there was no taxi, but a black Mercedes made the turn behind him. He turned onto Rue Emile Edde, then turned left two blocks farther on, and then took a quick right. The Mercedes had not turned onto Rue Emile Edde, and now there was no car behind him.

He started for the safe house.

Ten minutes later, Louie pulled behind an apartment building on Rue Makdissi and parked. He entered a service entrance at the rear of the building, climbed the stairs to the second floor, and took an elevator to the fifth floor. At the end of the hall, he stopped in front of apartment 57, unlocked the door, and entered. The apartment was sparsely furnished: a cheap copy of a painting of the Beirut shoreline and a travel poster advertising Middle East Airlines adorned the pale yellow walls. Stained green carpeting covered the floor. An ornate couch and two chairs were placed around a coffee table. A radio and a lamp sat on a small table at the left end of the couch. A large brass bowl filled with packs of cigarettes lay on the coffee table beside an ashtray. Three stools and a bar separated a small kitchen from the sitting room. One bedroom and a small bath completed the layout.

About twenty minutes later, a faint knock sounded at the door. Louie opened it to two men of medium height, shorter than Louie, with black hair and mustaches that grew down below the corners of their mouths. They both wore dark glasses; open-necked, short-sleeved shirts; and dark trousers.

"Ahlan," Louie said and smiled as he stepped aside to let them enter.

Both men grinned broadly, the whiteness of their teeth exaggerated by the blackness of their mustaches. They removed their sunglasses as they entered, putting their right hands over their hearts.

"Praise Allah that we find you well, Effendi," the first one said.

"Praise Allah that you are well, and may Allah bless your families," Louie said, motioning for them to sit.

The two men sat on the couch, and Louie, sitting opposite, opened a pack of cigarettes from the bowl and offered it. Both accepted, and taking a lighter from his suit pocket, Louie lit the cigarettes.

"My friends," he said, "we have a new target. He's a KGB officer, so he'll be well trained to look for you. His name is Alexander Petrov: married, with one child, a daughter, living with him and his wife, Tamara. An older son studies in Moscow. Here's what he and his wife look like." He took seven copies of a photograph out of his coat pocket. "It's four years old. Pass these out to the team.

"He'll probably go to the embassy tomorrow morning. You know they work half days on Saturdays. Try to pick him up as he leaves and take him home. Stay with him all weekend. Put him to bed each night. We want to know how he spends his free time and with whom he associates. Case his apartment building—I want to know everybody who lives in it. Make sure you're accurate about which families live in which apartments. You can use the same cars all weekend. That's it. Any questions? Any problems? Fuad, you? Abdul?"

"L'a, Effendi. No questions. But what do we do if we lose him?"

"You aren't going to lose him unless he has an agent meeting. If that happens, go back to his apartment building and wait for him to return. Note the time he arrives."

"And what if he meets someone? Do we stay on the Soviet?"

"No, take the guy he meets home and identify him, and then go back to Petrov's building and start again."

"D'accord, Effendi."

"OK. Let's meet here Sunday night at eleven. You should have him in bed by then. If not, I'll wait here until you arrive. Allah Ma'ak," Louie said. Go with God.

In the car after leaving the safe house, the two Lebanese surveillants talked about their case officer on the way to a bar to have a drink before they telephoned the other members of the surveillance team to meet them at eight the next morning.

They had worked for many case officers, but they especially liked this one. He had short-cropped curly black hair. His eyes were large and round, dark brown. Crinkles in the corners showed he laughed easily and often. But the lower part of his face was different. His lips were thin and turned down at the corners, and the shape of his jaw gave an appearance of hardness. They enjoyed laughing with him, but they did not want him to become angry.

They did not know his name.

More than a year before, when first introduced as the case officer who would direct the team, Louie had spent many hours with them. He rode with them on surveillance exercises to learn how they thought and where their instincts led them under various conditions. Once, he had directed them to surveil him for three hours. He wanted to see what they looked like from the target's perspective.

They stayed close to him the first two hours and let him see them for what they were. During the last hour, they backed off, hoping to convince him that he had lost them. Louie had walked many blocks during the last hour, changing sides of the streets often, and then had caught a taxi to a Maronite Catholic church. Inside, he had dipped his fingers in the holy water cupped within a marble pedestal near the entrance, crossed himself, and gone to a pew to kneel and pray briefly. Then he strolled around the church, seemingly aimlessly, until slipping quickly out a side exit. Hailing a taxi, he went to Hamra Street and there wandered in and out of shops until he was convinced the surveillance team had lost him. He stopped at a small outdoor café, drank a coffee, and smoked a cigarette before catching a taxi back to the embassy.

That night, at a meeting in a safe house with the seven-member team standing in a circle in the living room, each with a drink in his hand, Louie critiqued their performance. He praised them for much of it and criticized them for having lost him.

When he finished, Abdul, the team leader, placed his drink on the coffee table and stepped into the circle of men in front of Louie.

With great hilarity, and much spilling of whiskey on the team's part, Abdul placed both hands on Louie's shoulders and said, "Effendi, when you left the church and took a taxi to Hamra Street, you went into the shop of the tailor Gabriel. Then you went into the shop next door and stayed only a minute and a half before going to the café owned by the Frenchman Pierre. You drank a cup of coffee and smoked a cigarette. You then took a taxi to return to the embassy. Effendi"—he paused for a moment to add drama to his next statement—"the taxi you took was ours. Hussain here was driving it." He pointed to a man to his left. "He wore dark glasses and a kaffiyeh, and he told you he was an Alawi from Aleppo, Syria."

Louie stared at Abdul and, after a long silence, exclaimed, "Ya' Allah!" and doubled over with laughter. And they liked him for it.

CHAPTER 3

At 10:48 a.m. on Saturday, a man wearing a short-sleeved white shirt, black trousers, and sandals pushed a three-wheeled cart piled high with oranges up the south side of the Corniche. At a corner of the Corniche and a small street to the right, he stopped and set up shop. He placed a large handwritten sign at the top of the pile of oranges that read *Oranges* in English, French, and Arabic, as well as the price per kilo. He tried to hail passing cars to stop and buy his oranges, but the price was more than four times the cost of oranges in the city. No one stopped. He didn't want them to. From his corner, he could see the entrance of the Soviet embassy and the cars parked on the street in front of the walled compound.

Behind him, also on the south side of the Corniche, parked among other cars, sat a black Mercedes with two men in the front seat. Parked a half block ahead of the vendor, a taxi waited with a driver and a passenger in the back seat. At the south end of the Soviet-embassy street, two men in a parked dark gray Peugeot could see the embassy entrance and the entire street.

At approximately a quarter after noon, people began leaving the embassy. A man dressed in a dark blue blazer, gray slacks, and an open-necked white shirt exited at 12:32 p.m. and walked to a white Fiat parked across the street. He got in and drove to the corner, stopping to wait at the stop sign for an opening in the traffic. Standing less than ten meters from him, the orange vendor turned his head down and to the left and spoke softly into his collar.

"Nam," he said, Arabic for *yes* but the surveillance team's signal for "I see him."

The car turned right.

The vendor spoke again into his collar. "Wahad," he said, Arabic for *one*, but it meant "right turn" to the other team members.

When the white Fiat turned, the vendor saw the license plate and, speaking into his collar a third time, reported, "Khamsa, sab'a" (five, seven). The car's license plate had a designator number for the Soviet embassy and a personal number for the registered owner. The plate read *68*. When the team transmitted numbers on their radios, for each digit, they always used one number less than the actual number.

CIA trained the surveillance team to practice strict radio security. The station knew that the Soviet embassy monitored radio frequencies looking for telltale signs of transmissions from surveillance teams. When KGB officers began their routine to cleanse themselves before going to meet an agent, they often drove carefully preplanned, timed routes, right or left turns, or stops at exact times while the embassy listened to suspected surveillance-team frequencies. If the embassy heard no suspicious transmissions timed to coincide with changes in the KGB officer's route, and if the KGB officer himself had not seen any surveillance activity, he drove to a prearranged site to look for a signal, often simply a flowerpot in a colleague's apartment window. If it was there, it told him he was clean and could proceed to the agent meeting.

When the white Fiat made the right turn, the black Mercedes eased away from the curb. Waiting for two cars to come between it and the target, the Mercedes merged into the stream of traffic. The man in the passenger seat said, "Nam," into his microphone. The taxi driver, wearing a kaffiyeh and sporting a thick, drooping black mustache, waited for two cars to pass behind the Mercedes and then said, "Nam," and entered the traffic.

As the Fiat continued east on the Corniche, the passenger in the Mercedes did not call out the names of intersecting streets passed. Rather, at each intersection where the target did not turn, he rapped sharply on his microphone with a pencil. The *click, click, click* told the other team members how many blocks the target had traveled without turning.

The Fiat turned left on Rue Mossaitbe. The Mercedes

called out, "Arba," *four*, designating a "left turn," and followed the Fiat. But when the Mercedes made the turn, there were no cars between it and the target, and the Mercedes was only a block behind. The Mercedes passenger called, "Sifr," Arabic for *zero*, ordering, "Replace me." The passenger, a cigarette dangling from his lips, rapped the microphone once with a pencil.

The Mercedes turned right at the next corner and went to Rue Salim Salam, where it turned left to parallel the target on Rue Mossaitbe. The taxi turned left and was three blocks behind the target when it entered the street. It kept that distance. The men in the Mercedes counted the clicks emanating from the taxi as they monitored the taxi's surveillance of the target.

When the Fiat's brake lights came on, an indication the driver was going to stop or turn, the taxi sped up to close the distance between them. The Fiat turned right on Rue Hussein Medawar. Holding his microphone in his right hand, the driver of the taxi said, "Wahad," and raced to the corner just in time to see the target pull into a parking area under the second building on the right. The driver then said, "Shukran," *thank you*, signaling to the team that the target had stopped. The man in the rear seat jotted down the number as the taxi cruised slowly by the building.

Alexandr Alekseyevich Petrov lived at 1357 Rue Hussein Medawar.

The taxi continued past the building to the next intersection, where it parked and waited for the Mercedes, which arrived in a matter of minutes.

After Petrov had left the embassy, the orange vendor pushed his cart two and a half blocks farther on until he arrived at a stall selling fruit and vegetables. There, with great waving of arms and shouting of expletives, he sold his oranges for one-fifth the price that he had tried to sell them on the street. He told the stall owner to keep the cart, saying he would pick it up later.

As soon as the transaction was completed, the dark gray Peugeot pulled up at the curb. The orange vendor jumped in the back seat. As the car sped off, the orange vendor changed his shirt and trousers in the back seat and would emerge wearing a blue shirt and gray trousers.

Within minutes, the Peugeot arrived at the intersection where the Mercedes and the taxi waited. It parked, and all the men from the three cars had a brief conversation before the Peugeot left and took up a position one block west of Petrov's apartment building. From there, the three men in the car could see the entrance of Petrov's building.

Two hours later, the surveillance team's leader, Abdul, entered the apartment building and approached the desk of the concierge. He showed identification naming him as Mahmut Said Rahman, an inspector in the Deuxième Bureau, the Lebanese internal-security service. The concierge snapped to attention and said, "Yes, sir," over and over as Abdul ordered him to produce the names of all the residents of the building and their apartment numbers.

Abdul's brother was an officer of the Deuxième Bureau who had provided Abdul and another team member, Kamal, with identification documents from his office. Abdul's brother also traced names, developed background information, and provided automobile-ownership records for the surveillance team. In fact, he provided any police and internal-security services the station needed. The station gave Abdul $300 a month to pay his brother for his cooperation. His brother had never met a CIA officer.

Another team member, Fuad, also had a brother who provided support for the team. Fuad's brother managed a car-rental agency and allowed the team to use any of his cars it wanted. Consequently, the team members often changed cars several times a week, with Fuad's brother providing different license plates for them. The station gave Fuad $500 a month for his brother.

The team would observe Petrov's every movement for the next thirty-four hours.

CHAPTER 4

Late Monday afternoon, Jack Duncan and John Patrick O'Shea wandered into Brooks Moss's office to hear Louie report what the team had discovered from the weekend surveillance of Petrov.

"Sit down," Moss said. "Louie just got here too. The team got Petrov. Go on, Louie."

"Well," Louie said, glancing at notes he had made in a small notepad, "the team picked him up when he left the embassy about twelve thirty on Saturday afternoon and stayed with him until he turned out his lights about eleven thirty Sunday night."

Louie walked over to the four-by-six-foot aerial photograph of Beirut hanging on the wall to the right of Moss's desk. "He lives right here," he said, running his finger slowly along the map in the southern part of the city. He stopped, picked up a red thumbtack from a small dish on the corner of Moss's desk, and stuck it in the map. "It's 1357 Rue Hussein Medawar, fourth floor on the right, facing the street, apartment 401."

He walked back to the couch and sat down. "We got the names of all the residents and their apartment numbers, and we're checking them out with Abdul's brother. We should get the results tomorrow. There aren't any vacant apartments."

"The Petrovs stayed home all Saturday afternoon, but at seven thirty that evening, they went out to dinner. They took their daughter with them and ate at the place called Chez Ali, just off Hamra Street. They ordered a meze, and Petrov and his wife shared a carafe of white wine. But here's something interesting: As they left the restaurant, they ran into a couple. The women hugged and kissed, and Petrov and the man embraced. The other woman leaned over and kissed the Petrovs' daughter and gave her a hug. After chatting for a few minutes, they all walked across the street to a little outdoor café, where they ordered coffee and the men had a cognac. They sat there until just before midnight."

"We've got to know who they are," Moss said.

"Yeah, I know, Brooks. So one car of the team took the Petrovs home, and the other two cars took the other couple home. The other couple's car had Italian-embassy license plates, and Abdul's brother is going to check with the Ministry of Foreign Affairs to see who's driving it. We know their address and what apartment they're in."

"Good," Moss said, nodding.

"So," Louie continued, "on Sunday, the Petrovs stayed home. But at four in the afternoon, Petrov left and went to the outdoor café at Pigeon Rock. There he met with Morozov—the *Rezident*, mind you—Yuri Bagrichev, and Anatoly Burtsev, all KGB. They sat at a table by the sea, away from the other tables, and they started ordering vodka. They ordered lots of it."

"So Petrov had drinks with the chief of station, Andre Petrovich Morozov, huh?" Jack Duncan asked.

"Sure," Moss said. "If you were a rezident with a case officer whose father is a lieutenant general in the KGB, wouldn't you drink with him?"

"Lieutenant general?" Duncan said. "How do you know Petrov's father is a lieutenant general?"

"You told us," Moss said.

"No, what I said was that we know his father is high up in the KGB, but we don't know what his rank is."

"Oh. Perhaps when you said he was high ranking, *lieutenant general* just popped into my mind," Moss said. "In any case, please go on, Louie."

"OK. They sat there drinking until shortly after seven," Louie said. "The team took Petrov home, and while he walked OK, Abdul said he was weaving all over the place when he was driving. When he turned onto Rue Hussein Medawar, his right rear wheel ran over the curb. I would have loved to have had audio in his apartment when he walked in. Anyway, the Petrovs turned the lights off at ten forty-five. The team stayed around until midnight and then broke it off."

Jack Duncan then briefed the group about what he had found by studying the transcripts of the Soviet-embassy phone tap over the weekend. He said Petrov didn't seem to be very active. He didn't receive many calls or make many—at least, not when compared to other KGB officers.

"He has contact with two Lebanese journalists, both of them from leftist newspapers," Duncan said. "The conversations don't seem particularly warm or personal. But there's one guy we have to get—Petrov talks to him a lot. And they are obviously buddies. His name is Paolo Carli, and the Diplomatic List shows he's a first secretary in the Italian embassy. They seem to be very good friends. They usually speak in French, but Carli speaks English, also, and speaks it well. Sometimes they lapse into English. And I'll bet you guys a hundred bucks that the couple the Petrovs ran into after leaving the restaurant Saturday night were the Carlis."

"I'll bet so too," Moss and O'Shea said in unison.

"Good," Moss said. "Louie, run down that Italian-embassy license plate number to confirm it. If that's who it was, we'll get cables off to headquarters and Rome and get name traces. This could be a real break. There aren't many communists in the Italian Ministry of Foreign Affairs, so we should be able to get to this guy. If he's not reporting his contacts with Petrov, we'll have a handle on him, and if they're good friends, he might not be. But whether he is or not, he might be willing to work with us if he thinks we're out to help Petrov improve his life. We'll see. Good work, you guys."

At Friday-Evening Vespers, the embassy's air-conditioning system was on the blink. After Ellie poured the first round of drinks, Moss and the case officers removed their jackets and loosened their ties. The double windows behind Moss's desk were open, and a gentle breeze floated in from the sea.

Moss leaned back in his chair. "All right. Who was the smart-ass who telephoned my wife Wednesday evening and told her I said I would not be home for dinner?"

No one broke the silence that followed.

Finally, Peter Falin said, "Brooksie, obviously none of us would know who did such a thing, but that evening when we all left about seven, you were still here. You had sent us all out to do something that ensured none of us would be home for dinner. Whoever committed such a dastardly act was undoubtedly motivated by the thought that deep in your heart you probably really wanted to be with us and didn't want to go home for dinner either. It was, I'm sure, a camaraderie type of thing. You know, like bonding."

"Very funny. When I got home at eight thirty, Barbara had already eaten and my dinner was in the refrigerator."

"And I'm sure your first thought was of us, right, Brooksie?" O'Shea asked.

"Yeah, it really was, you jerks. OK, let's get down to business."

Jack Duncan slapped his knee as a great guffaw erupted from around the coffee table. It was Ellie's signal to enter and pour a second round.

"OK, that's enough," Moss said. "I want to know about Paolo Carli and who lives in Petrov's apartment building."

"I'll start," Louie said. "The Italian-embassy license plate checks out to be Paolo Carli. We've sent cables to headquarters and Rome, and he seems to be a good guy. He's known in the Italian Ministry of Foreign Affairs as a capable and polished diplomat. He comes from a respected family, and in fact, his father served two terms in the Chamber of Deputies, their version of our House of Representatives, as a member of the Christian Democratic Party. He's a rightist. Paolo studied two years at Eton in the UK and one year at the Sorbonne in France. He speaks English and French very well. It just so happens that he served in Paris at the same time Petrov was there. I'll bet that's where they met. If so, they've been friends for a long time. I had the embassy security officer check contact reports from embassy officers, and it turns out that Oscar Williams of the political section knows Paolo Carli and his wife well. They served together in Brussels some years ago, and the Williamses see them often socially. So we have easy access to him."

"Good," Moss said. "Tell us about the apartment building."

"Well," Louie said, "no vacant apartments. But we found something very interesting. The people who live across the hall from the Petrovs are none other than Nabil Khouri and his family."

"Who's that?" O'Shea asked.

"Well, it turns out that Nabil Khouri is the brother of Robert Khouri, an employee of this embassy. He's the driver for Bob Paine, the labor attaché. Nabil works for Olympic Airlines and just got a promotion. He wants to sell the apartment and buy a house."

"Great," Moss said. "Go buy the apartment."

"Go buy the apartment—just like that?" O'Shea asked.

"Yep, go buy the apartment. We'll put somebody in it. And then we'll sell it when the operation is over. Buy it as a representative of a Belgian company that does a lot of business in the Middle East. Explain to Nabil Khouri and the concierge that it's cheaper for your company to buy an apartment than it is to pay hotel costs for your people who travel here frequently. Tom"—he nodded to Tom Whiteside—"you have a phony Belgian passport. You make the purchase, and be sure to get some business cards made up that you can hand out.

"Jack, I want you to recruit Paolo Carli. I'll go see Oscar Williams and ask him to give a small dinner party and invite you and your wife and the Carlis. You can tell Carli that the State Department is conducting a survey around the world to find out what attitudes Soviet diplomats have about the countries they are serving in. By discerning that, the department may gain some impression of what type of reporting the Soviets are sending back to Moscow and how that might influence Soviet policy in that country. Tell him you've been asked to conduct that survey here and you're looking for people who have contact with Soviets. Let's see what he says—whether he volunteers Petrov's name.

"OK, let's get Ellie in here for one more round and call it a night. You guys have done well this week. Put the team back on Petrov. Who knows what we'll come up with next week?"

CHAPTER 5

Peggy Williams was pleased with her dinner table. The centerpiece of hyacinths was elegant, and the two tall, slender red candles on either side added a subtle touch. There were two wineglasses at each setting, the smaller for white wine, for the first course, and the larger for the Bordeaux, which would accompany the roast duck that Chandrika prepared so superbly. Chandrika was a gold mine. She was from Sri Lanka, and the Williamses had hired her when they were posted to Brussels. She had become part of the family, and they had taken her with them whenever they were transferred.

They were having the Carlis for dinner, old friends from their time in Brussels. Carlina Carli and Peggy were avid bridge players and good tennis partners at the club. The Carlis also knew Chandrika, so it would be a warm dinner party. The Duncans, from the embassy, were also coming. He, Jack, was a CIA officer, but Oscar had warned Chandrika not to mention it. She knew better than that—she had served with

Oscar in four posts and knew better than to refer to embassy officers as CIA. Jack's wife, Cindy, was a favorite of Peggy's. She was vivacious and fun and made every social evening livelier. Oscar told Peggy that Brooks Moss, another CIA officer in the embassy, had asked them to arrange this dinner so that Jack Duncan could meet Paolo Carli. Oscar didn't know why.

Promptly at 8:30 p.m., the Carlis arrived, Paolo with a large bouquet of long-stemmed roses. They were followed shortly by the Duncans. The dinner was superb and the conversation light and witty. Cindy Duncan brought the house down with her hilarious impersonation of Whoopi Goldberg.

After dinner, the men retired to the den with cigars and cognac, where the conversation became more serious and centered around the Israeli invasion of southern Lebanon. Paoli Carli did an excellent summation of the alignment of various United Nations members supportive of, or opposed to, the Israeli aggression. Jack Duncan said he had been given a curious assignment by the embassy: to try to discern what Soviet-embassy officers were reporting to Moscow about their impressions of the Israeli incursion. He explained that the State Department presumed that Soviet policy would be influenced by the reporting from their Beirut embassy. But, he said, "I don't know anyone in the Soviet Embassy, so I don't know where to start."

Paolo Carli took a long draw on his cigar and blew a thin stream of smoke toward the ceiling. He looked at Jack, took a sip of cognac, and said, "I have a Soviet friend. Perhaps I could ask him what they think. Moscow has been hesitant to comment on the incursion."

"Paolo, that would be very kind of you. Thank you for the offer. If you see your Soviet friend, please do ask him about their embassy impressions of the Israeli action. And if you'd like, call me, and we could meet for lunch."

The two men shook hands. The dinner party ended with embraces all around. The evening had been a success.

CHAPTER 6

At 9:40 a.m., Sabri Kassis, a member of the CIA station surveillance team, walked into the lobby of the building at 1357 Rue Hussein Medawar. The concierge, a middle-aged man with a patch over one eye, greeted him warmly. Sabri presented the concierge with a business card showing him to be Fuad Rizik, a representative of the Cedars Realty Firm. Sabri told the concierge he was canvassing the area looking for apartments for sale or rent for a foreign client who wanted to live in this area of Beirut. He asked whether anything was available in this building.

The concierge said, "We have nothing definitely available right now, but we do have a family that has expressed interest in selling their apartment. But it has not been listed yet."

"On what floor is the apartment?" Sabri asked. "My client doesn't want to be on the ground floor."

"The apartment is on the fourth floor, facing the street."

Sabri gave the concierge a hundred-pound note and said,

"I'll telephone you this evening, and you tell me when I can bring my client to meet the owner of that apartment."

"Shukran, Rais," the concierge said with a slight bow of his head.

The next evening, just before sunset, Sabri and Tom Whiteside were welcomed graciously into the apartment of Nabil Khouri. Over strong Arabic coffee, Sabri presented his real-estate representative card and introduced Tom Whiteside as Paul Vanderheuven, his Belgian client. Whiteside's business card identified him as a representative of a Brussels company, Middle East Development Inc., as did his passport. The CIA had made the passport. Paul Vanderheuven explained in French-accented English that his company had extensive investments and oil-exploration interests in Saudi Arabia and had a constant parade of their employees traveling from Brussels to Beirut to Riyadh. The company had decided it was economically wiser to buy or rent an apartment in Beirut than to pay hotel expenses. Whiteside didn't speak French, but he was an entertaining mimic of foreign accents—especially at parties.

Nabil Khouri said, "It is a frequent interest of foreign companies doing business in this part of the world. We have several other apartments in this building owned by foreign companies."

Whiteside wondered whether they might be owned by MI6, the KGB, or the French SDECE.

A selling price was quickly agreed on, with an agreement that Nabil Khouri would leave his telephone line in the apartment. Whiteside didn't care what the apartment cost, but telephone service was hard to come by in Beirut. Sabri agreed to present the contract in two days. The CIA now owned the apartment across the hall from Alexandr Alekseyevich Petrov and its telephone.

The brother of surveillance team member Abdul, an officer of the Deuxième Bureau, was a gold mine for the CIA station. He had gone to middle and secondary school with Mahmut Abu Rahman. Mahmut had made his career in the government telephone services and was a regional director of Beirut telephone exchanges. He could enter them all, go behind the boards, and do whatever he wanted.

At the request of Abdul, his brother had approached Mahmut and told him that he and several of his Deuxième Bureau colleagues had gone into a security business on the side and needed to be able to tap telephones in the city. For $300 a month, the CIA could tap any telephone in Beirut.

The Beirut station now had a tap on Alexandr Alekseyevich Petrov's telephone, and the device to record the calls would be located in the apartment across the hall from his apartment.

CHAPTER 7

At his desk at CIA headquarters in Langley, Virginia, Jack Wilson, the chief of the branch in the Soviet division of the clandestine service responsible for supporting CIA operations against Soviet targets in the Near East, closed the file and said to his deputy sitting opposite, "I think she looks great. She's just what Beirut is looking for. Get her ready to go, tell Beirut who we're sending, and ask them how they want her documented."

At Friday-Evening Vespers, after Ellie had poured the first round, Brooks Moss said, "I have an announcement."

"Yeah, yeah," Jack Duncan said. "We know, Brooksie. Only two more working days until Monday. What have you planned now to screw up our weekends?"

Moss waved his hand, dismissing Duncan, and said, "Arriving tomorrow at nineteen hundred hours on Olympic flight 226 is Tatiana O'Neill, thirty-eight years old, the same age as Petrov's wife, Tamara. She was born in Hong Kong to a Russian mother and an American father. She was married to a CIA officer who was killed in Colombia. No children. She's been in the company twelve years, mostly as an analyst and a Russian linguist. But she's been through the ops course at the farm.

"She'll have a US passport in the name of Elena Dubois, the wife of Lukas Dubois, an American who works for the Belgian company Middle East Development Inc. He spends most of his time in Saudi Arabia managing oil field surveys. Actually, her husband, Dubois, will be Ricky Novikov, one of our case officers in Vienna. He will come down here a couple of times a month to spend a few days in the apartment with Tatiana to establish her bona fides with the Petrovs. He'll also be available for us to run into Petrov. But he's got a full plate in Vienna, so he can't stay here for extended periods.

"Tom"—he pointed to Whiteside—"you pick her up tomorrow night at the airport. She has dark brown hair, five feet five. She'll wear dark glasses and a white blazer with a pale green blouse. Take her directly to the apartment. Introduce her to the concierge as the wife of a colleague in your company who will look after the apartment while her husband works in Saudi Arabia. Got it?"

"Of course I've got it. What do you think—I'd tell the concierge?"

"I don't know, but if you miss her at the airport, go defect or something, because I don't want you to come back to this station."

"Ellie, bring the vodka!" Louie Martelli yelled. "We're all going to say goodbye to Whiteside."

They all laughed, except Brooks Moss.

"Jerks," he muttered. "Let's go home."

CHAPTER

T om Whiteside was impressed. Tatiana was pretty. She had
a wide-eyed openness about her yet an air of sophistication
that made you think before you spoke to her. And she laughed
easily and heartily, putting you at ease. He liked her.

She had been well trained in the use of the recording
device, concealed in a poof at the foot of her bed, that would
capture on tape all the Petrov telephone conversations. The
station had moved an ample desk into her bedroom, where
she could work transcribing the tapes of the conversations. In
fact, the station had installed the recorder three days before
Tatiana arrived. Every time the Petrov phone had been picked
up, the recorder was activated. There was a full tape.

Tatiana would begin transcribing it in the morning.

Whiteside briefed her on their communications. He didn't
want to come to the apartment anymore because the Soviets
might recognize him. He showed her a hand-drawn map of a
small shopping arcade two blocks from her apartment. At the
end of the entrance of the lobby to the surrounding shops, an

elevator served small residential apartments two floors above the shops. Number 2D was a station safe house, and that's where they would meet every Monday morning at nine thirty.

Each day, to submit the transcriptions of the Petrov telephone tap, she would walk one block to the local post office.

Whiteside gave her a key to a postal box where she was to deposit her work every day before noon. The station had another key to the box.

If she wanted an emergency meeting, she was to call an embassy telephone number he gave her and ask for a Mr. Chapman. The woman answering would say, "I'm sorry. You must have the wrong number." The station secretary would check a box of three-by-five cards on her desk and see that a call for Chapman was to be given immediately to Tom Whiteside, and he, or another station officer, would be at the safe house in two hours.

The first transcription Tatiana submitted was unremarkable: lots of calls to and from embassy colleagues and their wives.

But it gave the station a clearer idea of the Petrovs' closest friends in the embassy. It was obvious that Tamara Petrov was a gossip who chatted with the other wives extensively about embassy personnel—who liked whom, who hated whom, and whom they suspected of having an affair. Useful grist for an intelligence service.

But there was one call that caught their attention. It was from Petrov's father. It went like this: "Papa, how are you? And a kiss to Mama."

"We are fine, son, and kisses and love to all of you. I called to tell you I talked to Yuri Ivanovich yesterday and he gave me bad news."

"What bad news, Papa?"

"You've been passed over for promotion again, and I don't understand. You are my son—I've talked to you and talked to you. Don't you pay attention? Your career is more important than your tennis game and your parties. You are my son, and they wonder why my son brings discredit on me."

"Oh, Papa, I do my best to honor your name and your reputation. It is important to our entire family. I do my best, I work hard, I worry about my career, and I want to bring honor and pride to you."

"Well, my boy, you'll be coming home on leave this summer. Then we'll talk. You tell Andre Petrovich of our conversation. You tell him I expect him to give you proper guidance—to teach you to be among the best and help guide your career."

"I'll tell him, Papa."

"Good. Goodbye."

CHAPTER 9

At eleven thirty on Thursday morning, a woman telephoned the American embassy and asked to speak to Mr. Chapman.

At 1:35 p.m., a light knock on the door of apartment 2D was answered by a mustachioed man, who said, "Come in, Tatiana. I'm Jack Duncan. Tom was not in the office when you called. We work together, so I came. Have a seat." He gestured to the couch. "I am very pleased to meet you, and we are delighted to have you here. May I serve you a coffee or a glass of wine? Are you OK? What's up?"

"Nothing for me, thank you, and thank you for coming. I am very glad to meet you also. No, I'm fine, but I have something I think the station should know about immediately. I haven't finished transcribing last night's tape, but there's a call in which the Petrovs agreed to go to Damascus on Saturday morning with two other couples from the embassy, to spend the weekend. Their apartment is going to be empty from Saturday morning until Sunday evening. I thought you should know."

"You bet we should know, Tatiana. That's great. Good for you. We'll want to go in there while they're away. You just caused five case officers and a branch chief to fall in love with you," Duncan said and smiled broadly.

"Wow," Tatiana said with a chuckle. "I'll call for an emergency meeting more often. What a windfall!"

"Now," Jack said, leaning over the coffee table, "Saturday morning, you go tell the concierge that later in the day, three men from your husband's company in Saudi Arabia are going to visit you. Tell him that you will serve them a midday meal and afternoon tea and that they will leave before the evening is over. Sometime early Saturday afternoon, three men are going to knock on your door. They will be a case officer and two audio techs. They will use your apartment to prepare to enter the Petrov apartment and place audio in most of his rooms. They should be in there five or six hours. Then they'll leave. We'll transmit the audio into your apartment. They'll bring a receiver and hook it up wherever you want it. We'll tell you later where to deliver the tapes, and we'll transcribe them in the station. You can't do it—you're only one person. Capisce?"

"I understand. This is exciting."

"It's an exciting job, darling," Duncan said as they shook hands.

As Duncan promised, shortly after noon on Saturday, Tatiana welcomed three men into her apartment.

One of the men said, "Tatiana, I'm Peter Falin, from the station. Welcome aboard. These two are audio techs from Athens. They arrived last night to do this entry for us. This one is Paul Craven"—he pointed to a tall man with a crooked smile—"and the ugly one is Mike Delaney." He pointed to the other one, who looked like he played tackle for Notre Dame. In fact, he *had* played tackle for Notre Dame, and he was an electrical engineer—as was his colleague, Craven.

They all shook hands and sat around the coffee table.

"Tatiana," Falin said, "we've telephoned the Petrov apartment, and no one answered. They're not home. Show her the key maker, Mike."

Delaney opened a small valise and pulled out a black object about the size of a cigar box. Protruding from one end was a thin narrow blade about six inches long.

"Tatiana," Falin said, "when we are ready, one of us will walk across the hall and stick the blade of this box into the Petrov door lock and quickly pull it out. It will take a nanosecond. The box will record digitally the markings of the lock. We'll come back here and make the key. It will take about fifteen minutes. And then we'll go in.

"These knuckle draggers"—he nodded to the audio techs— "will probably put four microphones in the apartment— perhaps two in the living room, one in a chandelier above the dining room table, one in the bedroom—and a transmitter. All will be powered from the apartment electrical circuit and transmitted to a receiver and recorder that we'll set up here before we leave. OK? Tom Whiteside will tell you how to get the recordings to us."

"OK. This is exciting, isn't it, Peter?" Tatiana asked.

"No, honey, this is the boring part."

Just before sunset, Peter Falin and the two techs returned to Tatiana's apartment. The job was done.

From his valise, Mike Delaney pulled out a bottle of single-malt Scotch whiskey, and as the two techs set up the receiving equipment and concealed it in a closet in Tatiana's kitchen, there was a great deal of backslapping and high-fiving. Tatiana loved it.

CHAPTER

J ack Duncan and Paolo Carli arrived at the restaurant at the same time.

"Thank you for inviting me, Jack," Paolo said as they were shown to a table on the veranda overlooking the sea at the Saint-George Hotel. The small choppy waves of the Mediterranean lapped at the base of the veranda, sunlight dancing on their crests.

Once they were seated, Paolo added, "I've been looking forward to seeing you again ever since our lovely evening together with the Williamses."

"It was a nice evening indeed," Duncan said. "And how is your charming wife?"

"She's well, as I hope your Cindy is. We are lucky men."

Over an arak, an exquisite mezze, and a carafe of wine, the two talked long into the afternoon, and the conversation turned to the Soviet friend Paolo had mentioned at the dinner party they had attended together.

"Yes, I asked my friend how the Soviet embassy was

handling the Israeli incursion into Lebanon. And he said—
his name is Sasha—that they are reporting the facts of the
aggression as they receive them, and how the aggression is
being reported by the Lebanese media, but pointing out to
Moscow that a strong Soviet condemnation of the Israeli
aggression will go far to increase Soviet influence in the Arab
world, at the expense of the Americans, who wouldn't dare
criticize the Israeli aggression."

"I think the Soviets have it right, and we should be
reporting the same thing. Is your Soviet friend Sasha Petrov?"
Duncan said, using his fork to transfer a few olives, a slice of
cheese, and a dolma from the mezze platter to his plate.

Paolo placed his glass on the table and leaned back in his
chair. His eyes widened, and he looked puzzled. "Yes, it is.
How do you know? Why do you ask me that?"

"I ask because Petrov's father is, or was, a high-ranking
KGB officer. We have always assumed Sasha was KGB also.
We have observed him for years. And your name has appeared
many times in reports about him."

"Si, naturalmente," Paolo said. "We are friends. We served
in Paris together. We became good friends. We like Sasha
and Tamara very much. We visited them in Damascus, and
we went to Cairo to see them. They came to Rome once and
spent a weekend with us. But during all these years, we didn't
know his father was in the KGB, and if Sasha is in the KGB,
we didn't know. And I'm not certain I care—should I?"

"I have no doubt that you didn't know, but—"

"Jack," Paolo said, "per favore. I don't think you are an American diplomat. You and I shouldn't know whether Sasha or his father is KGB, and we shouldn't care. That has nothing to do with our discussion of how the Soviet embassy is reporting about the Israeli incursion into southern Lebanon. Perhaps I shouldn't be here." He pushed his chair back, folded his napkin, and placed it on the table.

"I am a CIA officer, and my job is to recruit Soviets. Yes, you should be here. Don't get up." Duncan reached out and placed his hand on Paolo's arm. "Paolo, we know you. We know of the long history of your prestigious family. We know the reputation of your father as an esteemed and honorable politician in Rome. You are one of us. We have known for years that we could speak with you frankly, if that was ever necessary. It's now necessary. We simply want to be able to ask you what you know, and think, about your friend Sasha Petrov."

"Sasha is a kind, gentle man. I will talk with you about him but will do nothing to hurt him or put him in danger. You said it was necessary to speak to me now. Why now?"

Jack looked down and took a sip from his glass, wishing he hadn't said that. "Now? Because you said Petrov is a kind, gentle man. Paolo, one doesn't *join* the KGB—the Communist Party places you there whether you like it or not. Petrov's father, as a high-ranking KGB officer, would have his son assigned to the KGB because that's what he wanted, not necessarily what his son wanted. We think a kind, gentle man doesn't necessarily want to be a KGB officer, with a life of involvement in clandestine activities and espionage operations in which people's lives can be destroyed."

"But what do you care whether Sasha is in a career he doesn't want—what difference is it to the United States whether there is an unhappy Russian in the world? Your government wants to make all Russians unhappy. That's the Cold War," Paolo said.

"Yes, that's the Cold War, but there's more to it than one side making the other side unhappy. The Soviet Union is a dangerously armed, closed society. It is vitally important that the United States understands Soviet intentions and objectives well, because a misinterpretation of Soviet actions could very well bring about the type of deadly confrontation neither side wants. We have to know, not guess at, their intentions.

"There are Soviets, like Petrov, who could provide valuable insight into Soviet policy objectives—if not now, then later, as they rise to higher levels. But we must view such Soviets as human beings who have the same hopes and dreams as most human beings. And if their society cannot help them achieve their dreams, perhaps we can help them. We can help them fulfill their lives while at the same time asking them to help us avoid catastrophic mistakes in our dealings with their government that might destroy both our people. We would have no intention to harm them. To the contrary, we would want to improve the life of a man like Petrov and make available to him opportunities he would never have without our support.

"So we want to ask you now. Help us understand Sasha Petrov. Help us know him, to learn whether he may have a problem that we could help solve, in return for his cooperation to help us protect our two people. If he is not that person, he will never know that we have had any interest in him. Certainly, Paolo, we would do nothing to harm him."

Paolo sat silently for a few moments. He reached into the inside pocket of his blazer and took out a silver cigarette holder, opened it, and removed a cigarette. He allowed himself five cigarettes a day—and it was time for one of them now. Lighting the cigarette, he leaned back, looked at Jack for a long moment, and said, "I will talk to you about Sasha. I will try to help you understand whether he is the type of Soviet you are looking for. But I will not ever try to question him for secret information about his job, his embassy, or his government. I will not become a spy."

"We will never ask you to solicit that type of information from Petrov. We will only ask you about your impressions of him." Duncan extended his hand, and the two shook hands.

Over coffee, Duncan asked, "How would you and Carlina like a long weekend in Rhodes at our expense?"

"Carlina and I love Rhodes, but we don't need your largesse to go there."

"I know you don't. But we would like you to ask the Petrovs to go there for three or four days with you. If they accept, we will cover your expenses. Not theirs. We want to see how they react to the idea. Let's meet here for lunch next Friday at the same time."

"Va bene."

CHAPTER 11

"All right, girls, knock off the chatter," Brooks Moss said as he entered his office and walked to his seat at the coffee table, around which sat his five case officers.

"Hey, Brooksie," "Hi, boss," "Yeah, girls," the men muttered in return and smiled.

"I see Vespers have already started," Moss said, eyeing the glass of vodka on the table at his seat and a glass in front of each officer. "Gentlemen, I want to devote this entire meeting to our progress against our newest target, Petrov."

"There he goes again," said John Patrick O'Shea, seated at the end of the table to Moss's left. "At every Vespers, when Brooksie has had a taste of vodka, we are *gentlemen*. Before the vodka, it's usually *you damn people*, and this evening we were *girls* when he walked in. Now we are *gentlemen*. Ellie, bring in some more vodka!"

"All right, knock it off. Jack," Brooks said and nodded to Jack Duncan, sitting across the table, "bring us up to date. What progress have we made?"

Jack Duncan drew a pen and a notepad from the inner pocket of his suit coat. "OK, listen up. First, we got a cryptonym for Petrov. He is now Deadbeat in all our communications. We have surveilled his home and cased his apartment building. We know who lives in the building and found the apartment across the hall from Deadbeat is for sale. We bought it. The surveillance team picked up Deadbeat and his wife meeting with a couple from the Italian embassy. To make a long story short, they are long-term good friends, having served in Paris together. To make the story even shorter, I recruited the Italian. I think he is going to be a superb access agent.

"We have tapped Deadbeat's telephone, and when he and his wife went to Damascus for a couple of days, we went into his apartment and installed three microphones. The listening post is in the apartment across the hall. We concealed the recorder in a footstool.

"And, as you already know, headquarters has sent us a Russian-speaking female officer to occupy the apartment across the hall from Deadbeat and his wife. She will pose as the wife of an employee of a Belgian company that does business in Saudi Arabia. As do many companies, they wanted to buy an apartment here rather than pay hotel expenses for their people who are transiting. Her ostensible husband is a guy from Vienna station. He will come here from time to time, and we will introduce him to Deadbeat.

"So far, we got one interesting tidbit from the tel tap.

Deadbeat's father called him and told him he had been passed over for promotion again. He scolded Deadbeat for his lack of performance."

"That might be interesting," said Tom Whiteside, sitting to Duncan's left. "We can improve his job performance."

"We sure can," added Moss.

"Damn, this looks good," said Peter Falin, sitting at the end of the table opposite O'Shea. "We've got a running start on this one. Let's go get him."

"You're right, Peter," said Moss. "We just made a decision. Deadbeat is a primary target—let's go. Go home, everybody. Have a nice weekend. I'll be around all weekend." Nodding at Duncan, Moss said, "Jack, I'll be available anytime you want to see me this weekend. Don't hesitate."

CHAPTER 12

On Monday morning, when Brooks Moss entered the suite that housed the station's Soviet section, Ellie smiled at him from her desk outside his office. "Good morning, Brooks. You have a guest in your office. Jack has been here since before I came in."

"Good," said Moss. "Bring us two coffees. Good morning, Jack. What brings you here so early?"

"Good morning, Brooksie," Jack Duncan said. "I think we have struck gold. Let me read you the audio transcript Tatiana finished yesterday evening." He lit a cigarette. "You may recall that when I recruited Paolo Carli, I told him and his wife to invite the Deadbeats to spend a long weekend with them in Rhodes. Well, he did, and listen to the reaction. This is when Deadbeat came home from the embassy Friday evening.

"Tamara: Good news, Sasha. Carlina called me, and they want us to go to Rhodes with them for a long weekend. Isn't that great? We'll have a wonderful time. We've never been to a Greek island. I hear they are beautiful.

"Sasha: What foolishness, Tamara. You know we can't go to Rhodes for a long weekend. Who's going to pay for it? We can't afford it.

"Tamara, angrily: Why can't we afford it? The Kuznetsovs went to Crete for a week. Why can they afford it and we can't?

"Sasha: You know why. Igor is two ranks higher than I am, and he makes more money than I do.

"Tamara: I know, I know, but why is he two ranks higher than you? He's three years younger than you, and he entered the job four years after you. What's the matter with you? Everybody is more successful than you. What's going to happen to us?

"Sasha: I don't want to discuss it. You have no idea what I do in my work. Just shut up about it. We aren't going to Rhodes."

Duncan paused, resting the transcript in his lap. "What do you think of that, Brooksie?" he asked as he took another cigarette from a pack in his blazer and lit it.

After a long pause, Moss said, "Jack, the last time I was in headquarters, I was told that even though every CIA station in the world has been instructed to always have three Soviet targets under cultivation, in fact, we only make a recruitment pitch to about four percent of those targets a year. I think this is one of those targets we are going to pitch. So let's discuss how to structure the pitch. I want this guy recruited."

"Oh, Brooks, I forgot to mention something. Saturday

afternoon, Tatiana left her apartment just as Deadbeat's wife, Tamara, came out her door. The two greeted each other, and Tatiana spoke to her in Russian, saying she noticed that the name on her apartment door is in Russian. Tatiana told Tamara she was new in the area and did not know where she could find a grocery store, so Tamara invited Tatiana to go with her to the local grocery store. After buying the few items they needed, the two women returned to their apartment building together. There, Tamara invited Tatiana into her apartment, and the two had tea together.

"Brooksie, the two women seemed to hit it off. Tamara told Tatiana her husband is a political officer in the Soviet embassy, where they served, and told her all about their two children. She told Tatiana she doesn't like Beirut because she has no close friends in the embassy and doesn't know any Lebanese. She did say, by the way, that she does have one friend whose husband worked in the Italian embassy and that they served together in Paris. Tamara questioned Tatiana in detail about how she, an American, spoke fluent Russian, where her husband was, why she is here alone, when her husband is coming to visit, and so on. Tatiana told Tamara that her husband is coming next Monday for a few days before going on to Saudi Arabia, where he will stay for two or three weeks."

"Great," Moss said. "Let's get Novikov into Deadbeat next week. When is he arriving?"

"Sunday," Duncan, said running his hand through his brown hair, cut almost short enough to be considered a crew cut. "I'm going to pick him up at the airport Sunday morning about ten, take him directly to a safe house, let him read all the tel tap and audio transcripts, and brief him. Do you want to come along?"

"No," Moss said, "not to the airport, but tell me where, and I'll meet you at the safe house about eleven or eleven thirty."

"D'accord," Duncan said and blew a thin stream of cigarette smoke toward the ceiling.

CHAPTER 13

Sunday, about noon, Tom Whiteside picked up Tatiana, who was standing on a prearranged street corner, and took her to a safe house, where she was met by Jack Duncan, Brooks Moss, and Ricky Novikov, who had just arrived from Vienna.

"Meet your husband, Tatiana. His name is Ricky," Duncan said.

Novikov stood up and extended his hand to her. "My dear Tatiana, these men have told me nice things about you. I am glad we are married," he said with a chuckle.

"Ricky, you and I are going to make a KGB officer into an American spy. Welcome aboard," Tatiana said, laughing.

The group spent the next hour briefing Novikov and planning the introduction of Novikov to Deadbeat. They decided that Tatiana would invite Tamara and Deadbeat for drinks the next evening to introduce Novikov. A bottle of vodka would be on the coffee table.

The next evening, an hour after Tatiana and Novikov

had finished dinner, Tatiana went across the hall and invited Tamara and Deadbeat for a drink to meet her husband.

When Deadbeat and Tamara arrived, Tamara bearing a bowl of pistachios, Novikov jumped to his feet, extended his hand to Deadbeat, and, in English, said, "My name is Lukas, and I welcome you to our home. As humble as it may be, our hospitality is warm. Please sit down. I hope, sir, you speak English. Unfortunately, I do not speak Russian, but Tatiana does, if we need a translator."

Sitting on the couch next to Tamara, Deadbeat said, "Thank you, sir. I do speak English, but it is comforting that both our wives speak English and Russian if we need help. Thank you for your kind welcome, and please call me Sasha. I am very pleased to meet you. I must not be the first Russian you have met—I see the bottle of vodka on the table."

"Sasha," Novikov said, "I have met Russians before, but I have never had a drink with one. You must know that your people have an international reputation as the world's leading consumers of vodka. I like vodka, and we will share this bottle, if you would like. Our wives can help us survive and help us make our way to our bedrooms." He poured vodka into the four four-ounce glasses on the table.

"I understand you are an American—perhaps you prefer some other drink," Deadbeat said, raising his glass.

"Ah, we Americans come from all over the world. We

can be as irresponsible as anybody," Novikov said, raising his glass.

"To a better world," Deadbeat said and emptied his glass in one gulp.

Novikov followed suit, coughing and gagging slightly.

Tamara and Tatiana sipped from their glasses, looking at each other and shaking their heads at the men.

"Sasha," Novikov said as Deadbeat picked up the bottle of vodka and refilled their glasses, "you made a grand toast—'to a better world.' Both of our nations are trying to make a better world, but each has a different opinion of what that better world would be. Your country thinks communism will make a better world, and my country believes capitalism will provide the most for its people. Let's hope we never attack each other to see who's right."

Novikov took one swallow from his glass and then emptied the glass in a gulp, again coughing. Deadbeat chuckled, threw down his drink, and banged the empty glass on the table before reaching again for the vodka bottle.

Watching Deadbeat fill their glasses again, Novikov said, "Do you think the world realizes that if your country or mine misunderstands the intentions of the other and for mistaken reasons attacks the other, millions will die? We will destroy the world as we know it."

"Oh," Deadbeat said, "let's not think of such things. You are right—our countries can destroy the world."

"Tatiana," Tamara said, "let's you and I go to our apartment and have a cup of tea. There's nothing worse than the forebodings of two drunks. My God, these two will turn the earth into a fireball."

"Tamara," Novikov said, "don't leave us. It is people like you and Sasha who can ensure our two countries understand each other. Tatiana and I have no role to play in defending the earth. I am a businessman, an American working for a Belgian company. We have no influence in international understanding. But you and Sasha—Sasha is a diplomat; he has a role to play in our two countries understanding each other. He can inform his government of American intentions and the Americans of Soviet intentions. He can play an important role in ensuring neither country attacks the other because of false understanding of the other country's intentions. You are a lucky man, Sasha—your government has given you an important role to play."

"Lukas," Deadbeat, said refilling his and Novikov's glasses, "you exaggerate my importance. I am not an influential Soviet diplomat. I am a junior diplomat. I have no role in influencing the policies and actions of the Soviet Union."

"Yes, of course," Novikov said, "but you are young, you will rise in your country's hierarchy as you age, and your rank and importance will become significant. As I said, you are a lucky man."

"Sasha, he doesn't know. He's being kind," Tamara said. "We must go. It is getting late, and you must work tomorrow."

The men embraced, as did Tamara and Tatiana, and the Deadbeats departed. When the door closed, Tatiana and Novikov saluted each other, shook hands, and embraced.

CHAPTER 14

"Ellie," Moss said, "tell Jack Duncan to go get Novikov and bring him here. Also, tell Whiteside to join us when they arrive."

"Yes, sir."

An hour later, Duncan and Novikov arrived.

"Where in the hell did you have to go to get him—Cairo?" Moss said to Duncan, nodding to Novikov, as Whiteside walked into the office.

"I was taking a shower when he arrived," Novikov said.

"At ten in the morning?" Moss asked.

"Yeah, I had a bit of a hangover this morning, and it was a little difficult to get started," Novikov said.

"That sounds like good news," Whiteside said.

"It is," Duncan said. "I called Tatiana at five this morning and got her up to transcribe the tape of their evening last night with the Deadbeats. Here's the transcript. It is damned interesting. Ricky here can fill in the details."

After reading the transcript, Moss said, "Gentlemen, I'm

going to pitch Deadbeat. This meeting will be to determine where and when."

The following Wednesday, Tatiana invited Tamara to be her guest at a Friday-evening performance of a visiting Ukrainian ballet company. Tamara accepted with obvious enthusiasm.

Twenty minutes after the two wives had departed for the ballet, Brooks Moss rang the Deadbeats' doorbell.

When Deadbeat opened the door, Moss said in English, "Mr. Petrov, I am sorry to disturb you, but I am from the American embassy. May I speak with you?"

"What is it you want?" Deadbeat asked.

"May I come in? I wish to talk to you about the relations between our two countries," Moss said.

"No," Deadbeat said, "I am not authorized to discuss relations between my country and America. Go to our embassy and ask to meet with our ambassador." He started to close the door.

"Your father will be disappointed in you once again if you will not talk with me," Moss said, putting his hand on the door to stop Deadbeat from closing it.

"What do you know of my father?" Deadbeat asked as he stepped aside and motioned for Moss to enter.

Sitting on the couch across from Deadbeat, who sat in an overstuffed chair, Moss said, "Sasha, I am a CIA officer, and I do not come as an enemy. Through the years, beginning with your years in Paris, we have thought of you as an unusual Soviet. We know you are KGB, as is your father. For eleven years, interrupted by your two two-year assignments in Moscow, we have tried to understand you and have watched you mature in Damascus and Cairo. We are satisfied in our belief that you are a man of peace and a thoughtful and intelligent observer of relations between the communist world and the noncommunist world. We have also learned that your very successful and influential father is not satisfied with the progress of your career."

Deadbeat held up both hands. "Stop. If you are a CIA officer, you are here to convince me to betray my country and my people. You have chosen the wrong person to be a traitor."

"To the contrary," Moss said. "I am here to give you a unique opportunity to serve your country and the Russian people. We believe you are willing to risk your life to save the Russian people. Our two countries have the capability to destroy each other and kill millions of our people in the next hour. If the Soviet Union has no hostile intentions toward the United States, the world would be a safer place if all could be assured that the US was convinced of that, and would not launch a military attack against the Soviet Union because of a misunderstanding, not being well informed about Soviet intentions and plans. And the same for the Soviet Union. No war must be allowed because of a mistake. I am offering you the opportunity of a lifetime, to play a role, no matter how minor, to prevent such mistakes from occurring."

"And what, sir, do you expect me to be able to know of Soviet intentions and plans? I am a junior officer," Deadbeat said.

"Yes. But as a KGB officer, you will receive briefings on Soviet plans that no other Soviet, and certainly no American, will ever receive. We would expect you to keep us informed of Soviet plans and intentions as you know of them. Your job would be to ensure that we, the United States, draw no false conclusions from Soviet actions and make that earth-destructive mistake."

Deadbeat rubbed his hands together and stared at them before dropping them to his lap. Looking up, he said, "I am prepared to do my part. I want peace in the world as fervently as anyone you have ever known. But you must promise me one thing: my father must never know of our relationship."

"I will promise you more than that," Moss said. "We will make your career more successful than either your father or you ever imagined."

"Who will meet with me, and where will we meet?"

"I don't know," Moss said. "Someday when you come home from the embassy, a man will approach you as you get out of your car. He will say, 'Hello, Sasha. I bring greetings from your father.' He will hand you a piece of paper with a drawing of a corner where two streets intersect. You are to stand on that corner at the time designated on the piece of paper. That man will pick you up from that corner in a car described on the piece of paper. He will take you to a safe house, where the two of you will meet. That man will make proposals to you to improve the success of your career. He will make your professional performance more effective. And you will respond to his questions.

"Before we depart, you should know that we are prepared to put a monthly payment of American dollars for you in a numbered Swiss bank account. How does a monthly sum of one thousand dollars sound to you?"

Deadbeat stepped back, his eyes wide. "That amount, sir, is more than I earn now. You are very generous, sir."

"Not at all, Sasha," Moss said. "That is just an introductory amount. We will discuss that as our relationship develops. My only concern is what you will do with the money. Any change in your lifestyle will attract the attention of your colleagues. And that could be dangerous for you."

"I know," Deadbeat said. "I am a trained intelligence officer. I know the things to avoid. Please don't worry about that."

"Of course," Moss said. "And there's one more thing—perhaps the most important. What is your operational target?"

"Well, I belong to a unit that targets Palestinian resistance groups—the PFLP, the PFLP–General Command, Al-Saiqa, you know," Deadbeat said. "And we are very successful. Well, the unit is. I have not been very successful."

"I know that," Moss said, reaching into his coat pocket for a pack of cigarettes. He shook one out and offered the pack to Deadbeat, who declined. "But we can solve that. We will provide you with a couple of agents."

"Oh, *madre mia*," Deadbeat said. "Your help could make my career."

"Let's get started," Moss said.

The two men stood and shook hands. Both had tears in their eyes.

CHAPTER 15

Moss arrived back at his office before the Friday-Evening Vespers began. Sitting behind his desk, he said, "Ellie, come in here and bring your dictation pad. And close the door. I'm going to send a cable to headquarters."

Ellie sat in the straight-backed chair in front of Moss's desk, pen and pad at the ready.

"You know the slugs that go on the cable, so I'm just going to dictate the message. Start with 'Deadbeat was recruited this date.'"

Ellie jumped up, threw her pad and pen in the air, and yelled, "Hot dog!" as the office door opened and Jack Duncan, Louie Martelli, and Peter Falin walked in.

"What the hell's going on?" Duncan said. "Do we get a day off this week or something?"

"Brooksie got Deadbeat!" Ellie yelled, dancing around the chair she had been sitting on, her black hair swirling across her face.

"Hey, boss, well done," Falin said as Martelli stepped in

front of him, pushed him out of the way, and shook hands with Moss.

"OK, you guys, sit down. Ellie, go get the guys some vodka, and pull that office chair up to the table and join us," Moss said as he grabbed the straight-backed chair in front of his desk and pulled it to the coffee table for Ellie.

John Patrick O'Shea and Tom Whiteside walked in and joined the celebration.

"My God, boss," O'Shea said. "Damn, you do make a contribution. I thought you just told us what to do."

"I do: shut up and sit down," Moss said, joining in the laughter around the table.

"Maladetz," Whiteside said—"well done" in Russian.

"All right, girls," Moss said, "now comes the hard part. We're going to make Deadbeat the best damn case officer in the KGB *Rezidentura*. So let's get started."

Moss reached into his blazer pocket and pulled out a pack of cigarettes, shook one out, and lit it with a lighter lying on the coffee table. He inhaled deeply and blew a thin stream of smoke toward the ceiling. "We are going to give Deadbeat one of our Palestinian agents. Louie, you and John Patrick handle a couple of Palestinian agents—tell us about them."

"Well," Martelli said, "we'd better talk to Billy. He runs the terrorist branch, and the agent I'm running belongs to him, not us, the Soviet branch. The guy's crypto is Abupenman. He's the administrative officer for the PFLP. He's a fantastic agent. He attends every serious meeting the PFLP leadership holds, and he takes the minutes of all the meetings. I get a copy of them. They include all their operational planning, the targets of their next operation, when it's going to take place, and who is going to be involved. The guy is invaluable. That's why Billy isn't going to let him go."

"I don't want Billy to let him go," Moss said. "We are going to broaden his access. We'll make him a more valuable agent, reporting on KGB interests and activities, as well as on the PFLP. We'll double his value for Billy. I'll talk to Billy— he's a good guy."

"Jack," Moss said, "you and Whiteside create how Deadbeat will present his new target to the Rezident. Figure out how the cover story will explain how the two met, and how, when, and where they have met since, and start making Deadbeat submit contact reports on how he is developing Abu-what's-his-name and how he finally recruits him. We'll discuss later what kind of false information we'll have the Palestinian report to the KGB. I'll be in tomorrow morning, Jack. You and Tom come in and brief me on what you two have decided. One last drink, girls, and then we'll go home."

CHAPTER 16

At 2:20 a.m., the phone rang, waking Moss from a deep sleep.

"Hello … Oh, hello, Ralph. What's up? Why are you calling me this time of the morning?"

"Get here as quickly as possible." The caller hung up.

When Ralph Moore, the CIA chief of station in Beirut, issued an order, the troops said, "Yes, sir," and saluted. Moss got up to dress.

In the station conference room in the embassy, Moore was joined by his deputy and the three branch chiefs. Sitting at the head of the conference table, Moore banged the table with his fist and said in loud, angry voice, "Louie Martelli was killed tonight!"

A roar erupted from the four men.

Moss, who had a glass in his hand from the makeshift bar in the corner, stood up and threw the glass against the wall.

The chief of the terrorist branch, Billy Longdale, also stood. "By God, I've got a new target! I'm going to kill somebody. I've got nine case officers in my branch, and we're going to be on the street tonight looking for a target. And I damned well know where to look."

"All right, all right, calm down. Sit down. I'll tell you what happened and what we are going to do about it," Moore said.

"As you know, Billy," Moore said, "Louie had a car pickup meeting tonight with that penetration we have in Al-Saiqa. As always in a car pickup, you had two guys staked out where they could see the pickup site. They were parked about half a block north of the site. As Louie approached, they blinked their lights, signaling 'all clear,' and Louie pulled up at the curb where the wog was standing, but instead of getting into the front passenger seat, the guy walked around to Louie's door and pulled it open. While he was doing that, a car pulled out of an alley about twenty meters from the front of Louie's car and pulled up face-to-face with Louie's car. Three men jumped out: two from the front seat and one from the back. That one stood and held the back door open. They obviously intended to kidnap Louie. By this time, the agent had Louie outside the car. But as the two men from the other car approached, Louie hit the agent and knocked him down. The first man from the other car grabbed Louie by the front of his coat, and Louie hit him, knocking him up against the car, and the guy went down on his knees. With that, the second guy from the other car shot Louie. Louie went down on his back. The man stood over Louie and shot him two more times. The four got in the other car and took off. Our guys picked Louie up and put him in their car. They took him to the hospital, where he was pronounced dead. That's where the body is now."

There was total silence at the table. A tear rolled down Billy Longdale's face.

"Now I'll tell you what I am going to do," Moore said. "I'm going to issue weapons tomorrow morning—the nine-millimeter Browning to every officer, and I want a submachine gun in every operational car. As you know, I have liaison with the chief of Lebanese Internal Security Forces. I'm going to see him this morning and tell him the following: 'I want the Lebanese army to go into the Palestinian refugee camps and apprehend every one of the twenty-five to thirty Al-Saiqa gunmen. I don't care about their families.' And if he won't do that, I'm going to tell him to tell his president that without the full support of the Lebanese government, he should know that the CIA will recommend to the president of the United States that we overthrow his government."

"Now, wait a minute, Ralph," said Tony Dragos, the Greek American deputy chief of station. "You are about to instigate a major international crisis. You've got to remember that Al-Saiqa is a Palestinian Baathist political and military faction created and controlled by Syria. If the Lebanese grab or shoot every member of Al-Saiqa in the refugee camps, Syria may very well invade Lebanon to overthrow the government. However, I think Syria might not react to the Lebanese arrest of those actually involved in Louie's death, because not to acquiesce to that would bring down the wrath of the CIA and the US government. Assad in Damascus wants no part of that. He's having enough problems keeping the lid on Syria without having the Americans mucking about, increasing his problems possibly to the breaking point. Let's go after the perpetrators and not Al-Saiqa as an organization."

All three branch chiefs nodded in agreement, and the chief of station said, "Tony, you are absolutely right." He ran his right hand over his dark brown hair, above his graying sideburns.

To Moss, Moore suddenly looked older. He hadn't noticed before the wrinkles around his eyes. His broad shoulders seemed to sag.

Straightening up, Moore said, "Yes, you are right, and as a matter of fact, it might be more effective, with greater impact, if Al-Saiqa realizes that we know who was involved in the killing of Louie. That means that the CIA has other penetrations of Al-Saiqa. For the rest of their existence, they will sit around their conference tables looking at each other, wondering who's the American spy. It also tells them that obviously everything they plan in the future, all their operations, will be known to the Americans. Al-Saiqa will never be the same again. Gentlemen, Louie performed his last patriotic act. God bless him."

"Amen," the men around the table mumbled.

For the CIA, the leader of Al-Saiqa, Zuheir Mohsen, was a marked man for ordering the kidnapping and killing of Louie Martelli.

Nineteen days later, the president of Lebanon sent three security police officers into the Shatila refugee camp on the southern edge of Beirut to meet with Zuheir Mohsen. They carried a message and a photograph. The message was "From the president: Within the next twenty-four hours, turn over the four members of Al-Saiqa who were involved in the killing of the CIA officer." The Lebanese gave Mohsen the names of those wanted, which had been provided by the CIA.

The police officers also showed Mohsen an aerial photograph of the Shatila camp, highlighting the area that Al-Saiqa personnel and their families occupied. The police told Mohsen as they stood to depart, "The president said to tell you that he is under great pressure from the United States. And if you don't give us those four men within twenty-four hours, he will order an air strike on the Al-Saiqa area of Shatila within forty-eight hours."

The men were handed over to the Lebanese authorities the next morning. At their trials, the shooter of Martelli was sentenced to twenty-five years in prison, and the other three men were sentenced to fifteen years each. Who would know when the shooter was released from prison on orders from Damascus?

Six months later, Zuheir Mohsen was gunned down in the hallway of the luxury hotel in which he was staying in Cannes. His killer was never identified.

CHAPTER 17

T amara answered the telephone, expressed warm greetings, and said, "Just a minute. Sasha, take the telephone. It's your father."

"Hello, my son. I called to tell you that I am very proud of you. Your recent, very important success is much the talk in the office here."

Deadbeat was teary when he hung up the phone. His father was a lieutenant general in the KGB. When he talked about "the office here," Deadbeat knew his father was talking about the highest levels of KGB headquarters in Moscow.

Deadbeat had recruited a Palestinian who was the administrative director of the PFLP. His success was highly praised in the Rezidentura and well recognized at KGB headquarters. He also had another Palestinian under cultivation, and it looked like he was going to recruit him also. He did.

Eight months after Moss recruited him in Beirut, Deadbeat received orders transferring him to Prague as deputy chief of the rezidentura. Deadbeat was delighted—it meant a promotion for him. He was also deeply grateful to the CIA for the abrupt change in his career.

Deadbeat's transfer to Prague also delighted the CIA. It would increase his access to KGB relations with another Warsaw Pact intelligence service and the operational program, successes and failures, of that satellite service. But meeting with Deadbeat in the hostile ambiance of a communist nation presented problems. The Czech internal-security service and its surveillance capabilities were well known in Western intelligence circles.

A month before Deadbeat was scheduled to leave Beirut, the CIA sent a case officer from Prague to introduce Deadbeat to the plans for clandestine contact with him in Prague.

The CIA had learned that their officers in Prague were under surveillance about 75 percent of the time over a two-year assignment. They could not contact, develop, and recruit agents in the country: The security services were ubiquitous. They had hundreds of teams available to surveil not only the personnel of foreign embassies but also hundreds of their own citizens every day. One could be arrested for having an unauthorized contact with a foreigner.

The CIA and other Western intelligence services were forced, therefore, to rely on agents they could recruit among Czechs who were serving abroad—Czech-embassy personnel were the primary targets. Once those agents were transferred back to Prague, the Western intelligence services lost contact with them until they again traveled out of Czechoslovakia or were again transferred abroad.

But the CIA had studied the practices and patterns of Czech surveillance and discovered a way to manipulate a surveillance team to make a clandestine contact with an agent without being observed by a surveillance team. They had observed that the typical Czech surveillance team had three cars and seven surveillants on foot. The foot surveillants put four people behind the target and three across the street. The first surveillant usually stayed fifteen to twenty-five steps behind the target, depending on the density of the pedestrian traffic. The lead surveillant across the street stayed a little behind, parallel to the target.

The first principle of the clandestine contact was that a surveillant must never see the CIA officer or the agent pass something to the other. Each passage would be one way—the CIA officer to the agent, or the agent to the CIA officer, but never an exchange between the two.

The second principle was that a surveillant must never see the agent's face. Therefore, every contact site had to be a place where the agent could pass or receive a package and disappear. Each site needed to have an escape route that would take the agent from the immediate area.

If the contact point were six or eight steps from a corner that the CIA officer would turn approaching the site, the exchange—the "brush pass"—could be made between the agent and the CIA officer before the lead surveillant turned the corner. When the surveillant did make the turn, he would see only the CIA officer twelve to fifteen steps ahead of him. The agent would have departed using his escape route.

For two weeks, the CIA officer from Prague and Deadbeat practiced the brush pass. The training lasted two weeks because the CIA officer from Prague had to find the appropriate sites in Beirut to practice the exercise, the place of the actual passing of a packet from one to the other.

In Prague, Deadbeat would be issued a rollover camera—that is, a camera embedded in a fountain pen. Seen lying on a desk, it would not be suspicious. Palmed in the hand, it could be swept over a written document to photograph each page as fast as the hand could move.

The packet he would pass to the CIA officer at a brush contact would be the size of a pack of cigarettes and hold three rolls of film specially made by the CIA for the camera. Each roll could make seventy-two photographs. Therefore, the agent could pass photographs of 216 pages of classified documents at each contact.

CHAPTER

For the first six months Deadbeat was in Prague, he had twelve brush contacts with the CIA officer. In six of those brush contacts, Deadbeat passed more than two hundred photographs of pages of KGB classified documents. In the other six contacts, the CIA passed Deadbeat money, requirements, and new rolls of film. The CIA was highly pleased with Deadbeat's performance. He showed excellent judgment in selecting the documents he would photograph, the lifestyle he reported to CIA was reserved and cautious, and the Rezident seemed to be pleased with his performance.

On a Monday morning, Deadbeat's father was called into the office of the director of the KGB First Chief Directorate, the organ of the KGB responsible for foreign intelligence operations. The director politely asked Deadbeat's father to be seated and offered him a cigarette, which he accepted.

"Yuri," the director said, "I have some very bad news for you. We have received information from a penetration of the CIA that your son has been recruited by the CIA."

Deadbeat's father slumped in his chair, his eyes filled with tears, and his face became pale.

"You know what we must do. We will bring him home and put him under arrest. He will be tried and sentenced to death. I am very sorry, and I wish I didn't have to tell you this. I will do anything I can to help you and your family."

Deadbeat's father straightened in his chair, took out a handkerchief, and wiped his eyes. "Sergei, this is impossible to believe. But I know you wouldn't tell me this if it weren't true. You know my son, Sasha, is in Prague and he is the deputy chief of the rezidentura. I ask you a favor from the bottom of my heart. Don't have him arrested in Prague by the Czechs and sent home in chains. It would kill his mother. Let me go to Prague and bring him back here. He will not resist anything I tell him to do. When we arrive in Moscow, I will take him directly to headquarters and turn him over. Please let me do this. I beg you."

Sergei Smirnov sat silently. He reached across his desk and placed his hand on that of Deadbeat's father.

"Yuri Petrov," he said, "this is a highly unusual request. I could lose my job agreeing to such a thing. But you and I have known each other for twenty-seven years. We are like brothers. I know Sasha, and he is a good boy. This breaks my heart. I am going to grant your request. I will arrange for a military aircraft to fly you to Prague and bring you back with Sasha."

The meeting ended. Two days later, Yuri Petrov was on a Soviet air force plane to Prague.

In Prague, he confronted his son, and Deadbeat confessed to his father, explaining between sobs that he'd accepted CIA overtures because the CIA could help him in his career and finally make his father proud of him. Father and son wept and embraced. The Prague KGB rezidentura had not been informed of the KGB's intention to arrest Deadbeat and return him to Moscow.

The morning after his arrival in Prague, Yuri Petrov put his son; his son's wife, Tamara; and their daughter in a Soviet-embassy diplomatic licensed automobile and drove to the German border. At the same time, Yuri's wife and Deadbeat's son were boarding a train in Moscow to Helsinki. They were armed with diplomatic passports provided by Lieutenant General Yuri Petrov.

At the Czech-German border, the Czech border guards noted the diplomatic license plates of the car driven by Yuri Ivanovich Petrov and waved the car through the border post. At the German border, authorities noted the car's license plates and checked the passports of the occupants. They also waved the car through the border post.

Yuri Petrov drove the hundred miles to Frankfurt. After entering the city, he stopped the car and pulled from his coat pocket a small map of the city. He then drove a short distance and pulled to the curb of Lohrberg Park. There he told Deadbeat to come with him and asked Tamara and her daughter to remain in the car. Petrov and his son walked about one hundred meters to a man sitting on a bench reading a newspaper.

When the two Russians were a few meters from him, the man lowered the newspaper and said, "My God, Yuri, it's been sixteen years. How are you, my old friend? It is wonderful to see you." He stood to greet him.

"Hello, Brooks," Petrov said. "It has indeed been sixteen years. How have you been?"

The two men embraced.

When Petrov stepped back, he said, "Brooks, I want you to meet my son, Sasha."

Brooks extended his hand to Deadbeat and said, "Hello, Sasha." Turning to Petrov, he said, "Yuri, Sasha and I know each other. Welcome to the free world, Sasha."

Deadbeat and his family, along with his father and mother, were taken to the United States and resettled in Madison, Wisconsin; documented with new names; and provided with cover stories of their backgrounds. Yuri Petrov died in 2010 and his wife a year later. Deadbeat's daughter and son both graduated from the University of Wisconsin and married, and each provided Deadbeat and Tamara with two grandchildren.

EPILOGUE

Aldrich "Rick" Ames was arrested by the FBI on espionage charges on February 21, 1994, in Arlington, Virginia.

At the time of his arrest, Ames was a thirty-one-year veteran of the CIA who had been spying for the Russians since April 16, 1985, when he went to the Soviet embassy in Washington, DC, and offered his services to the KGB. It was a deadly offer.

The true-name files of CIA agents were kept in the offices of the counterintelligence staff of the Soviet division of the CIA clandestine service. Personnel of the division were not allowed to enter those offices without special clearances. That is where Aldrich Ames worked. He had access to the true-name files of all Soviets who had been recruited by the CIA.

Ames passed to the KGB the identities of eleven KGB officers who were serving as CIA penetrations of the KGB. Ten of those KGB officers were executed by the Soviet government. One escaped and was resettled in the United States under an alias and a fictitious background.

Ames is serving a life sentence in prison without provision for parole. He will die in prison.

Printed in the United States
by Baker & Taylor Publisher Services